The Lightbridge Method

A Stewards of Octarma Tale

of Short Proportions

R.H. Polden

I0588546

National Library of Australia Cataloguing-in-Publication entry:
Creator: Polden, R.H., author.
Title: The Lightbridge Method: A Stewards of Octarma Tale
ISBN: 9780648681656 (Paperback)
Subjects: Science Fiction/Humour Novella.

Tale Publishing
Melbourne Victoria

Tale

With thanks to Kim Smith and Peta Culverhouse for their editing and mentorship throughout this project and whose apparent thorough knowledge of ner'er-do-wells I feel best left unexplored.

Subrium Universe Tourism Board
Qurkition Galaxy

Outer-Brim

Inner-Brim

Systems

Outer-Brim

Aertion
Bertion
Certion
Dertion
Eertion
Ftertion
Gertion
Iertion
Kertion
Lertion
Mertion
Nertion
Oertion
Omertion
Pertion
Phertion
Psertion
Rertion
Sertion
Taertion
Tertion
Uertion
Xertion
Zertion

Aertion 82
Aertion 12
Zertion 11

©Half-Arsed Harry Intergalatic Mapping Corp. Where close enough, IS good enough.

Contents

T–6 It's All for Effect

"DO I ASK, WHY PEOPLE TEND TO LEAVE A LOCATION AS SOON AS YOU ARRIVE?"

The well-dressed humanoid figure of Jonathan Milarum stood on the bridge of his spaceship the *Beletheia* and stared out at the planet below. Deep in thought, Jonathan couldn't shake the feeling that his life was meant for something more than working for the family business — an entertainer at children's events — whilst under strict instructions from his older sister, Felicity, to keep his twin brother, Nickolas, out of trouble. Hell, he didn't even really like children much, and to his mind Nickolas was more than old enough, and certainly ugly enough, to look out for himself. But alas, this was his life, and he was stuck with it. His thoughts were broken a few moments later by the voice of his ship's primary computer, M011y, informing the crew that they are about to land.

"So what jolly job is this one M011y?" Jonathan asked as the out-of-shape figure of his twin appeared on the bridge and handed him a cocktail that Nickolas had just fetched from what was statistically the hardest working device on the ship — the universal cocktail maker — installed conveniently[1] adjacent to Nickolas' primary seat on the bridge.

"Who cares. Just another bunch of thankless brats we have to attempt to entertain." Nickolas finished his own cocktail, sensed his brother didn't want his, grabbed it back and made short work of it.

"As much as it pains me t0 say, I c0ncur with y0ur deadbeat brother, a totally p0intless exercise." M011y was more interested in

---

[1] A little too convenient for Jonathan's liking.

scanning the planet below for 'business' opportunities.

"Now, come now team, let's keep it together. It's the only job we have booked this shift so far, and anyway, we need to show our new apprentice the ropes." Jonathan secretly agreed with Nickolas and M011y but tried to keep things professional.

"It's Berkley Bing-Beekeson sir, and may I say it's a privilege to be working with you two," spouted the young, smartly dressed[2], stick-thin humanoid sitting awkwardly on one of the bridge console stools.

"So, Berkley. Are you jolly well excited to be on your first job my good man?" Jonathan looked down fondly at the young fellow.

"Absolutely, it's a dream come true just to be here … but to be assigned to the Milarum brothers whose family owns the business, it's amazing!" replied an obviously excited Berkley.

"Look Beeksy, I don't have the time nor the energy to give you the details of why this job will crush your dreams, and then move onto your soul, so I will let him do it." Nickolas smirked as he motioned to his brother.

"Pardon? And my name is Berkley Bing-Beekeson sir." Berkley looked surprised.

"Sure Beeksy … And anyway, what happened to the old apprentice M011y?" Nickolas ignored Berkley completely.

"Went 0ff to join the suicide sh0ck tr00pers of Pertion 42. She said it w0uld be less dangerous than working with you two."

"I don't blame the girl. Okay let's get this over and done with. M011y do the honours would you." At Nickolas's command, M011y e-dressed both the twins in their worn and totally underappreciated clown outfits, and e-dressed Berkley in an overtight, low-cut, pink-coloured, sparkly assistant uniform which was obviously used by their last assistant.

Nickolas finished his drink, laughed at how ridiculous Berkley

---

[2] It's All For Effect (IAFE) employees were always smartly dressed by the organisation's rules of the business. This was to take the focus away from the fact that their performances were anything but.

looked, groaned a bit, then moaned, "Hit it!"

M011y transported the twins, Berkley and some props directly to the job's presentation stage.

"Good children of Xertion 9. Greetings, salutations, or as the peace-loving tribe of natives on Certion 23 would say, 'I hope you brats all end up in soup!'" Nickolas bowed as the children all yelled and applauded.

"Excuse me?" the one adult in attendance blurted out.

"So, who here loves jolly soup!" Jonathan added quickly as he shot a scolding look at Nickolas, as the audience, oblivious to the exchange, continued to applaud.

"And what a less than zero cycle this is. We are totally unexcited to be here," Nickolas shouted though clenched teeth as he directed Berkley to do a little ad hoc dance to the sound of blaring electronic music.

"Are you having a laugh young man?" the adult shouted.

"Indeed. It's all part of the jolly splendid act, and your name is?" Jonathan asked in a calm tone as if he had done the same thing many times previously.

"It is Miss Pimppopp, the children's teacher," the homely looking middle-aged female answered in a matter-of-fact way.

"Okay Miss Pimple Popper, prepare to be amazed! Because for my first trick, I am going to saw my assistant in half!" Nickolas shouted to the audience.

"You're … what?" Berkley looked surprised.

"Look, just remember your training and follow my lead," Nickolas growled.

"But I was never taught that one! I'm scared!" Berkley shot back.

"You should be Beeksy. You should be. Now show the crowd a little more cleavage and get into the box." Nickolas gave him an evil grin as Jonathan helped Berkley into the prop.

The boos only commenced with their third bungled trick[3]—pulling a grombit[4] out of an e-hat — where the e-hat backfired allowing the alarmed grombit[5]to escape into the crowd.

Nickolas, sensing he was losing the audience[6], took to the front of the stage.

"Who here would like to see a shooting star? Assistant? Please pass me the remarkable wonder out of my magical satchel!" Nickolas motioned to Berkley to pass him an item out of the ratty bag they had brought.

Berkley reached into the satchel and passed Nickolas a little black box marked EITD.

"No, not that remarkable wonder. The other one." Nickolas motioned quickly to Berkley.

Berkley handed Nickolas another device. This one was in the shape of a small bottle.

"Girls and boys. Behold! The bottle of 'limitless star power'!" Nickolas boomed.

"But, before we continue. I must ask all adults to leave the room. For their own safety." Nickolas shot a glance directly at Miss Pimppopp.

"Why on green Vertion 11 would I do that?" Miss Pimppopp shot back.

"Do I ask why people tend to leave a location as soon as you arrive? For your safety." Nickolas shot her a look that could have possibly sunk a thousand ships.

"Safety? Well, I never!" Miss Pimppopp continued to complain loudly as Jonathan gently guided her into the next room.

During this distraction, a child entranced by the mysterious

---

[3] Rest assured Beeksy only suffered a minor injury during the 'sawing in half' act.

[4] The grombit is a small animal native to Hertion 5. With its white fluffy coat, large ears, twitchy nose, and a tail that resembled a powder puff, they were endearing creatures and popular pets.

[5] The downside was, when startled, their defence mechanism was to exude a scent that most of the inhabitants in the Quirktion galaxy found extremely noxious. Fortunately for the twins, the inhabitants of Xertion 9 have little sense of smell.

[6] Nickolas and Jonathan had lost more crowds at this point than a one-armed piper.

object Berkley had loosely stuffed back into the bag, raced up to the stage and touched the black box. The child promptly disappeared.

Unfortunately, no one noticed[7], as with a flick of his wrist and a puff of smoke Nickolas opened the glass bottle which lit up and captivated the audience with glowing lights in ever-changing psychedelic colours.

"Okay sweet children … look into the bottle … look into the bottle …no, don't look around the bottle … look into the bottle." The children did as they were bid and with a snap of his fingers Nickolas declared, "Right, you're under!"

The children in the room now sat in deadly silence, clearly under the influence of some type of trance.

"Now, listen up you little horrors. You are having a wonderful time. You love our show and will henceforth show us the appreciation we deserve via tips, positive reviews, and applause every time any employee of our company walks into a room. For ever after. Understood?" Nickolas said firmly.

"Yes, we understand," droned the children in a collective response.

"And another thing. You will each now make it your life's mission to destroy Miss Pimppopp's life," Nickolas added quickly with a broad smile as Jonathan reappeared back in the room.

"3-2-1 … and … you're back in the room." Nickolas snapped his fingers again.

The entire room broke out in applause.

"You really should not do that brother. Especially the jolly bit about the teacher," Jonathan said to Nickolas.

"Harmless fun. You know the device only works on little brats[8], and most of them could not organise their way out of a wet paper e-bag,"

---

[7] Which was a shame really, as it certainly was a moment that could have been captured by the brothers of evidence that their 'magic' worked and may have won the audience over.
[8] And believe me, Nickolas had attempted to use the bottle of 'limitless star power" many a time on bar keepers and loan sharks up and down the galaxy. Sadly, no luck so far.

"Is what we do even legal? It certainly wasn't in my training," Berkley quipped.

"Oh, I'm sure it's legal Beeksy ... somewhere." Nickolas laughed.

The brothers, along with a clearly shocked Berkley, made their way back to the now landed *Beletheia* and moments later were sipping cocktails in celebration of what Nickolas proudly toasted as 'a job rather poorly done.'

"Okay M011y, what's the next jolly job?" Jonathan asked.

"Still awaiting confirmation. A computer glitch back at head office apparently, which I can't be bothered helping to fix." M011y preferred to use her runtime on more stimulating — not usually of a legal nature — pursuits.

"Well hooray for the black art of technology. This gives us time to check our other employment opportunities." Nickolas brought up a screen on the primary display and started rubbing his hands with glee.

T–5 Opportunity Knocks

"THAT'S LIFE FOR YOU ISN'T IT."

The *Beletheia* was now wandering aimlessly through space, flying towards something or other, or to be technical, some random planet in the Xertion sector, which formed part of the larger Qurkition galaxy. M011y didn't much care either way, she was busy making bets with fellow computers in the area, while the twins took the opportunity in-between HQ computer glitches to investigate other forms of 'revenue streams'. It was only from these various side hustles that kept Nickolas vaguely interested in life at all. His latest hobby saw the brothers moonlighting as entertainment consultants for large events under the flashy name of their latest extremely well-marketed enterprise — The Lightbridge Method™[9].

"So, what do we have here then?" Nickolas continued to scroll down the screen marked recent enquiries.

"Shouldn't we be waiting for our next job," Berkley interrupted.

"Huh? What? Oh, you're still here Beeksy. Look, why don't you go and give the ship's exterior a nice polish. We will call you when we need you," Nickolas said as Jonathan simply shook his head.

"But we are in open space." Berkley looked shocked.

"Exactly," Nickolas replied flatly.

"Okay what about this jolly job? … 'Entertainment needed for

---

[9] The Lightbridge Method™ was growing into a big hit, thanks to the marketing company Nickolas used for all his promotional needs — 'Don't-Quote-Us-On-That Inc.'. The twins were popular because they were cheap, ethically challenged, and somewhat liberal in their views when it came to safety checks — they never did any.

the upcoming Interstellar Procrastination Summit … we will discuss looping back to you with the details at the last moment'," Jonathan read as he scratched his head.

"Bloody crank callers," Nickolas commented.

"Oh! Rather." Jonathan felt embarrassed he didn't get it sooner.

"Okay, what about this? 'Clean up at this moon-cycles Intergalactic Vacuum Cleaning Conference by providing spotless, dust-free, fun entertainment for our guests. Looking for acts that don't suck!'"

Nickolas looked at his brother blankly.

"Okay, this is not getting us anywhere. M011y please find us the best paying legit job," Nickolas quipped.

"That's easy. Zertion 11," M011y replied.

"Zertion 11? The same jolly Zertion 11 that is home to the notorious Soprarmio family?" Jonathan suddenly looked worried.

"The very same. It's paying maj0r-credits th0ugh," M011y replied

"How many credits we talkin'?" Nickolas' nose for a quick credit started to twitch.

"Y0u kn0w all th0se gambling and bar tab debts y0u have strewn 0ver the galaxy?"

"All too well," Nickolas shuddered at the thought.

"Enough to pay them all 0ff then s0me," came the reply.

"I'm listening," said Nickolas.

"You can't jolly well be serious? The Soprarmio family are one of the most powerful organised crime families in the sector," Jonathan warned.

"So, I'm thinking they will pay in cold hard credits. Anyhow, we need the dosh and I need the distraction," Nickolas said matter-of-factly.

"I have a jolly well bad feeling about this." This was hardly an uncommon feeling when Jonathan dealt with his brother's various schemes.

"I don't. If we can deal with screaming brats all sun-cycle, how hard can it be taking candy from some hardened criminals?" Nickolas was already sold.

"Indeed, but hardened criminals are usually armed with a tad more than fizzy pop and confectionary," Jonathan replied anxiously.

"M011y, please reach out to Zertion 11 and setup a meet and greet." Nickolas ignored his brother while ordering himself another cocktail.

"Whatever. But y0u had better deal with th1s first," M011y brought up an image of a dutiful looking humanoid-shaped, blue mechanoid on a secondary display screen.

"Oh, it's Dr Fuddy Duddy himself. What's up Fuds!" Nickolas said sarcastically.

"I hope you're not drinking while on duty Milarum. Your family owns the business but there are still rules and regulations that we all follow. I have no option but to put you on report." The mechanoid had already commenced the latest of a long line of reports.

"It's pronounced 'recommendation' Fuds!" Nickolas lifted his glass in salute.

"And stop calling me Fuds! My name is Scheduling Coordinator 90889,"

"Yes, of course. How can we jolly well assist you 90889? Do you have our next job perhaps?" Jonathan butted in.

"Your next job is a birth-cycle party on Zertion 87. It's commencing shortly, so please proceed directly to these coordinates I have just transmitted. I trust you will aim to please," Scheduling Coordinator 90889 said.

"I wouldn't think so Fuds! We mostly aim NOT to please. And we reach this aim almost every time." Nickolas rewarded Fuds with a finger gun and a wink.

Scheduling Coordinator 90889 shook his robotic head, processed if anything else Nickolas had done during this transmission that could be reported, confirmed twenty-six instances, smiled, then terminated the transmission.

"Well, my good Beeksy, enough motley coddling or whatever. Time for you to strike out on your own." Nickolas smirked.

"But I have only done one job, and it hardly went well!" Berkley moaned.

"Don't sell yourself short. It went splendidly. Now, M011y you heard Fuds! Set course for Zertion 87, drop off our master entertainer here, then swing over to Zertion 11." Nickolas gave the clearly rattled Berkley a high five.

"It did?" Berkley replied.

"Look Beeksy, you will be fine, just do what I taught you, and if you get into a tight spot, then use this." Nickolas casually threw him the bottle of 'limitless star power!'

"But you taught me nothing!" Berkley exclaimed.

"That's life for you isn't it. But consider this … who really teaches who?" Nickolas pondered this question aloud to the general confusion of all.

Jonathan almost felt sorry for Berkley as he gave his brother a look of someone who had been left so high and so dry, he might have preferred to polish the exterior of the ship after all.

T-4 Zertion 11

"WELL, THAT'S A LEVEL OF INCOMPETENCE I'VE NEVER SEEN BEFORE."

Zertion 11 barely rated as a planet at all given its small size. Not only that, but most of the planet was uninhabitable given the surface was entirely covered in ice. In fact, the only thing of significance on Zertion 11 was a large dome-like structure that protected the inhabitants within against the hostile external elements — which sometimes even included the weather. But given it was also the home to one of the largest organised crime families in the sector — the Soprarmios — elements of an internal nature were usually just as hostile.

"Don't worry about good old Beeksy brother, I'm sure he will be fine. He did get basic training after all, right M0l1y?" Nickolas glanced at his brother, completely disregarding the worried look on his face.

"Wh0 kn0ws, and 1 can't be b0thered checking either," M0l1y replied.

"Oh, splendid! Let's hope nothing ghastly befalls him and he gives them a good show," replied Jonathan.

"Look at it this way brother, our star rating can't get any lower," Nickolas replied in a satisfied tone.

"That is true. I think the kindest review we have received lately was, 'well, that's a level of incompetence I've never seen before'," Jonathan recounted.

"Exactly. And as our beloved sister always reminds us, 'IAFE takes pride in entertaining children across the entire quality spectrum,' we just specialise in the lowest end of that range." Nickolas laughed.

"Commencing 0ur descent t0 Zertion 11 n0w," M0l1y announced.

As the *Beletheia* started its landing sequence, they could not help but notice an exceptionally large, grey spacecraft instantly recognisable by its markings as a Gambunyepio spaceship hovering above the city dome, which coincidentally was the other notable morally challenged crime family from the Zertion sector.

"Oh, jolly good. Seems we arrived just in time for the Zertion mob summit. Spiffing marvellous." Jonathan tried to keep the sarcasm out of his tone. He failed.

"Interesting. The Gambunyepio spaceship cOmputers tOld me it was tOwed here. And currently crewless," M011y added.

"Oh, double bloody spiffing now." Jonathan glanced at his brother, who didn't seem to be concerned at all.

Shortly afterwards, the *Beletheia* landed in one of the space docks connected to, but located just outside the dome, and the twins were greeted by two shady looking characters dressed in perfectly tailored 28-piece black suits.

"Welcome to Soprarmio Prime Supreme Ones! Me name's Carlo and dis is also Carlo. Da Boss Overlord is expecting yah," the first Carlo spouted as they directed the twins to follow them towards a sparklingly white marble, triangular, high-rise building which was, unsurprisingly, the largest building within the dome.

As they walked through the busy streets, the twins noted that the rest of the buildings within the dome were made up of run-down, tired-looking, off-brown, single-storey dwellings.

"Classic power move this." Nickolas was impressed.

Once within the solidly built, yet tasteless, white marble building, they took the turbo lift to the top floor and entered into a spacious, marble-floored, open-planned space.

Vinnie Da Boss Soprarmio sat behind his large, tasteless, marble desk that dominated the room, close to one end of the building. It wasn't lost on the twins that Da Boss's desk was also close to a least three potential exit strategies if need arose, with a turbo lift to his right, a set of stairs to his left, and behind him a window that led directly out to what looked like a small balcony with a large spacecraft hanger attached.

His office area was crammed with many over-sized black couches and what looked like guards. They were all surrounding a short figure currently on his knees in front of Da Boss.

"Hold it here fellas. Da Boss Overlord will see yah in a tick. Just dealing with some joker." The Carlos grinned in unison.

Da Boss Overlord: Say, look, I'm not an unreasonable man, Jack the Knife, but this is the second chance that I've given you. See?

Jack the Knife: But I'm a poor man boss.

Da Boss Overlord: Yes, but it's not just me, see. A lot of people depend on these extortion credits. My new spacecraft doesn't just fuel itself you know.

Jack the Knife: I will make it up to you next sun-cycle. I promise.

Da Boss Overlord: Say, I understand, I do. But I really can't give you a another chance ... sets a bad example. I'm so sorry.

Da Boss Overlord turns to his guards: Say, would you please rub him out? ... Outside of course. This flooring is still new.

Jack the Knife screams: Oh no! Take all my beloved knives as payment. Take all of them!

Da Boss Overlord thought about this: Say, that's a good idea. Go to his house, bump off his family, then take all his knives as payment.

Jack the Knife falls to the floor on bended knee gripping his hands together and yelled: Mercy!

Da Boss Overlord: Say, I do wish you'd think ahead Jack old boy, it would have saved all this unpleasantness. See?

Nickolas and Jonathan watched on with facial expressions ranging from worry to indifference[10] as the guards dragged a whimpering Jack the Knife off towards the stairs.

Da Boss Overlord turned to the twins and smiled. "Say. Da

---

[10] No credits for guessing which brother had what expression.

entertainment consultants have arrived. Good sun-cycle to yah both."

Jonathan stepped forward. "And a fine sun-cycle to you Mr Soprarmio. My name is Jonathan Milarum and may I introduce my twin brother, Nickolas. We are indeed the entertainment consultants you requested, at your service your excellency."

"At yah service indeed. Say, I do love politeness. Respect will get you a long way here. Say, walk with me." Vinnie motioned for the twins to follow him out onto his balcony.

"So, what type of entertainment do you require your excellency?" Nickolas enquired so politely that is brother glanced at him in disbelief.

"A celebration, see, and a dual one at that. Victory over those no-good rats the Gambunyepio's. We gave them an offer they couldn't refuse" — Da Boss Overlord laughed — "and a celebration of my birth-cycle."

"My congratulations to you Overlord. On both counts. So, sir, it seems you will require the entire Lightbridge™ experience?" Nickolas continued as he mentally started to tally up the bill.

"I want you to illuminate our dome here with a light and music show for the ages, see? Then, as a grand finale, I would like this spaceship rubbed out." He pointed upwards towards the Gambunyepio spaceship they'd passed on route.

"Destroy that ruddy spaceship?" Jonathan winced as he looked up.

"Assuming that won't be a problem gentleman." Vinnie continued to gaze upon the Gambunyepio ship overhead.

"Well, here's is the jolly thing …," Jonathan muttered.

"The jolly *thing* alright, is that destroying ships is our speciality." Nickolas gave his brother an annoyed glance.

"Splendid. I want your weapons to launch from the planet's surface. I want it to be a grand spectacle. A show of power. Say, I'd like you to live stream the event to the entire sector," Da Boss Overlord boomed.

"We will aim to please!" Nickolas replied before his brother could even consider inserting some sanity into this conversation.

"Splendid. You get it. You two kids are hired. And credits are no issue. C.O.D. of course, see." He smiled as he led them back inside.

"We are honoured for the opportunity." Nickolas tried to give a bow of respect but failed.

"Good, good. Say, then you had better hop to it. The celebration is in two sun-cycles. Apologies for the late notice, but the consultant who we had originally booked ... let's just say ... disappointed me, see." Da Boss Overlord motioned to one of this security monitors showing a live feed of an eight-legged orange creature stretched out on some type of rack.

"We will *stretch* ourselves to provide the best celebration you have ever seen then." Nickolas smirked as his brother simply shook his head.

"Say, you two are a hoot. Now Carlo and Carlo here will help you with the details. I have some other matters to attend too, see." He smiled as his guards dragged in his next appointment.

The twins quickly made their way back to board the *Beletheia,* and were commencing their launch sequence, when Jonathan couldn't hold his tongue any longer.

"You've completely gone around the jolly twist this time. An entire city's dome lit up with sights and sound might be possible, but we *don't* have the weaponry to destroy a ship of that size. Especially if they want the weapons to launch from various locations around the city, in perfect sync."

"I am sure M011y will figure something out," Nickolas shrugged.

"And the weapons required to pull this off?" Jonathan continued to press the point.

"Oh, don't worry your ugly little head about that dear brother. I know a place and by a spot of luck it's also in this sector."

T-3 Weapons Outpost 8953

"I TAKE IT YOU EITHER DON'T GET OUT MUCH, OR YOU'RE SIMPLY A MORON."

Things had obviously turned rather hostile towards poor IAFE apprentice entertainer Berkley Bing-Beekeson. When the brothers returned to Zertion 87 to fetch him, they found him running for his life with what looked like an entire tribe of angry warrior children hot on his tail. It took some fancy navigating by M011y to swoop down and transport poor Berkley off the planet's surface before he ended up in hot water. Literally.

"What jolly well happened down there?" Jonathan handed a clearly shaken Berkley some type of drink.

"Yes, my old chum Beeksy, do tell." Nickolas smiled as sipped his latest cocktail.

"The show! The show!" Berkley blurted out. Still out of breath.

"Went badly. yes, we see that. Why didn't you use the bottle of 'unlimited power'?" Nickolas asked.

"I tried."

"You forgot to turn it on, didn't you?" Nickolas shook his head.

"You had to turn it on? I was never inducted! They smashed it to pieces in the end and were about to do the same to me before you rescued me." Berkley by now was a wreck of nervous proportions.

"Oh, I wouldn't worry. I have plenty of spares, but the cost will be deducted from your first pay, I'm afraid. M011y, remind me to visit my old pal Pauli Wauli next time I'm home to replenish my stock." Nickolas chuckled at the thought.

"I nearly got killed out there," Berkley cried.

"And let that be a lesson for you," Nickolas replied.

"And what lesson would that be?" Berkley spat.

"A pretty good one." Nickolas, by now, had lost all interest in the conversation.

"Indeed. Now onwards and upwards, I say my dear Berkley." Jonathan butted in. "And in that vein, dearest brother, we have accepted a job working for the most dangerous crime family in this sector. Where is this magical place you mentioned that will be willing to hand over enough missiles, free of charge I might add, to destroy a spaceship that has obviously been obtained via some type of turf war?"

"Old Muck-a-muck here is way ahead of you, as usual. M011y set course to these coordinates." Nickolas punched the details into the navigational computer muttering *you pompous git* under his breath.

"0h, with p1easure. At 1ast something interesting to d0." The *Beletheia* changed course so violently that poor Berkley lost his footing and crashed to the floor.

Nickolas laughed at Berkley as he stepped over him on route to order another cocktail. The brothers knew from experience that when M011y changed course, she changed course *suddenly*.

"You're having a jolly laugh, right? Jonathan studied the new coordinates.

"Not unless the laugh is on them," Nickolas offered his brother another drink.

"You know a visHamogus weapons outpost has security cameras everywhere. Even cameras that monitor those cameras. They will spot us coming from half a galaxy away and given our families current relations. They would hardly hesitate turning those weapons on us old boy."

"Look, I'm sure old Franklin, and our old school chum, Thomas don't man their own security cameras, and as for that drunken old flame of yours, Eloise, she is too busy single-handily purchasing every designer piece of purple clothing in the galaxy, wedged in-between drinking herself to death, dear bother."

Jonathan caught himself slightly blushing. "Yes. Rather."

"And anyway, given it's a disposal outpost, the security is nowhere near as tight as usual. Trust me, the good old Muck-a-muck here." Nickolas grinned.

"I do wish you would stop using that ghastly nickname[11]," Jonathan spouted.

"And anyway, you're forgetting we have two secret weapons," Nickolas continued, ignoring his brothers last comment.

"Secret weapons?" Jonathan looked confused.

"Good old super-brain M011y here and him—" Nickolas motioned towards Berkley.

"What? Berkley? I mean we can't expect him to jolly well help us steal weapons now, can we?"

"He is here to learn, right brother?"

"Yes but—"

"And they won't recognise him, will they?"

"I guess not."

"So, leave it with Muck-a-muck here to work out the finer deets, which starts with you brother heading down to the cargo hold and making room for a few missiles."

"How many is a few?"

"About one hundred few." Nickolas looked pleased with himself.

Jonathan knew from experience, which was often painful, that it was just easier to go with the flow at this point, so he simply shrugged his shoulders, gave Berkley a sorrowful glance and headed off in the direction of the cargo hold as instructed.

"Now Beeksy. This is what I have in mind." The broader Nickolas' smile the larger the dread in the pit of Berkley's stomach became.

---

[11] Nickolas had surmised long ago that the only good nickname was a nickname you gave yourself. Giving himself the heroic nickname Muck-a-muck, stopped anyone else giving him one that he didn't fancy — which given his personality, was a certainty — and secondly, Nickolas also claimed it was the perfect party conversation icebreaker. Jonathan had never witnessed it breaking much ice, especially with the ladies.

***

A short while later, the *Beletheia* landed next to a run-down old factory on the outskirts of a tired looking industrial estate on the planet Zertion 31.

Not wasting any time, the figure of IAFE apprentice Berkley Bing-Beekeson disembarked from the ship and made his way hastily yet reluctantly to reception.

"Well, hello my good man, what a lovely sun-cycle," Berkley was so nervous he barely got the words out.

"Considering I am female and it's stinking hot, this, and pretty much every cycle on this awful bloody planet, I take it you either don't get out much, or you're simply a moron," came the sarcastic reply from a clearly dishevelled, yet attractive female humanoid figure.

"Huh, what?" Berkley was taken aback.

"So, a moron then, I see. But where are my manners? Welcome to dirty, stinking visHamogus weapons outpost 8953. My name is Helga. How can I be of assistance?"

"Greetings valued employee Helga. My name is Berkley visHamogus and I'm here for a surprise routine safety inspection," Berkley, staying on script, blurted out.

The mention of the visHamogus name did have some effect as Helga endeavoured to straighten her well-battered uniform. She attempted anyway.

"So, you're a visHamogus?" came the obvious question.

"Fourth cousin, twice removed from Thomas and Eloise. Love them both like cousins," came the reply.

"You don't by any chance have any identification on you, even a recent family photo would do." There was still a hint of suspicion in her voice.

"Absolutely, and great question, feel free to check it out on your computer. It should also have a record of my unscheduled visit." Berkley scanned his hand on the offered ID device.

"Oh, I intend to." But as fast as the smug sneer appeared on

Helga's unwashed face, it disappeared even quicker when her ID computer came back confirming that Berkley was not only a visHamogus, but also a high ranking one at that, and was to be given full access to the facility, no questions asked.

"So, I would like to start with a full weapons inspection." Berkley surmised from her face that M011y's divine electronic intervention had worked.

"You do realise this is a factory seconds weapons outlet. Basically, where useless weapons come to die?" Helga said.

"Oh yes, exactly. I'd like to start with inspecting the missiles in order of inventory total," Berkley stated in a tone that was almost convincing.

"That would be easy then. The only missiles we have in stock that number more than a handful each are the Diggers 0.1s. Both worthless and useless, so quite the winning combination," Helga commented.

"Perfect. Let's start with them. Please wheel out a hundred of them out front so I can inspect them personally while enjoying the lovely mid-cycle light."

"So, you want to safety inspect 100 highly volatile missiles … missiles, mind you, that never made it out of prototype stage in the scorching mid-cycle heat in a vacant customer parking lot? If that sounds like a sane request to you, then you must be on some strong medication. And if you are, I'd like some." Helga looked perplexed.

"That is my request." Berkley tried to look as serious as possible.

"Something sounds bloody dodgy here, but fine. Whatever. I will have the service droids wheel them out shortly." Helga shrugged her shoulders and disappeared out the back.

A short time later, container after container of missiles were wheeled out of the factory by a legion of security guards and were opened for inspection as instructed.

"So, what are you looking for sir?" one of the droids asked Berkley as he started looking them over.

"Defects."

"But sir, they are all defective. That is why they are here in the first place. What the—" The droid sensed a large noise behind him.

The droids all looked around. To their amazement, they saw a large black spacecraft de-cloak, while firing up its engines.

"Hold! Imposter! Shoot them!" Helga screamed as she raced out of the front office, weapon drawn. "I checked with regional command. No such person exists. They must have hacked our local security database," she screamed. The security droids quickly drew their weapons and starting firing upon the *Beletheia*, which returned fire, stunning many of them.

Berkley, not standing around on ceremony, and knowing the jig was up, made a mad scramble towards the *Beletheia*. While in the background, the missiles were being beamed abroad the ship.

Berkley , now scared out of his mind, was sprinting towards the ship when he felt a sharp pain to his leg.

"I've been hit!" he shouted as he fell into the ship as its hatch closed.

The factory workers stopped firing and watched as the *Beletheia* took off and made its way quickly into the planet's upper orbit.

"Who would go to this amount of trouble to steal a bunch of defective weapons we couldn't even give away anyway?" one of the droids asked Helga.

"I have no idea but do scan the news communications for a mass weapon malfunctioning disaster. I'm sure we will find out then," Helga replied with a wry grin on her face.

T-2 The Setup

"DRY RUNS? SAFETY CHECKS? HILARIOUS!"

The *Beletheia* didn't waste time returning to Zertion 11 and was in the process of landing when Nickolas, who was experiencing such a good vibe about this new enterprise, had spent the entire trip formulating some draft resignation communications and was now running them past Jonathan.

"Dearest Big Sis,

I'd like to say it is us, not you, but I'd be lying. It is you … and our crummy company. We quit! Kind regards. Your brothers,

OR

To Whom it may concern,

Byeee!

J & N."

"Very droll, brother. Hadn't we better stick to the jolly matter at hand and actually complete the job before any thoughts of grandeur and quitting kick in?"

"I don't have time for such matters brother. Oh, and how is our little soldier, all patched up and ready to go plant us some missiles?" Nickolas glanced at Berkley, who limped onto the bridge looking decidedly worse for wear.

"If memory serves. When I applied for this position it specifically stated in the application, no moonlighting for personal gain." Berkley wasn't best pleased.

"I wouldn't worry about that, because you, Beeksy, are not being paid in credits. You are being paid in knowledge. The most powerful currency of all." Nickolas smirked.

"Aren't you two even going to help me?"

"And ruin a great learning opportunity for you? No fear. Once we disembark, M011y will help you install those missiles in the optimum locations throughout the dome to ensure the most dramatic explosion. My brother and I will be thinking of you though. While enjoying a working lunch with our employer." Nickolas tried to keep a straight face.

"What about running some tests, not to mention safety. The IAFE handbook clearly states—" But before Berkley got an opportunity to start quoting the IAFE work health and safety policies, Nickolas motioned to him to shut his mouth on pain of possible death.

"Safety, schmafty. It's not as though some fancy fireworks, lighting, pumping music or destroying innocent spaceships is going to permanently damage their tiny freezing planet or endanger any lives."

"True." Jonathan agreed.

Carlo and Carlo were again there to greet their arrival and escorted the twins back to Vinnie Da Boss Overlord's command centre where, it seemed, he was dealing with another delicate matter.

Da Boss Overlord: I have told you, Lou the Lighter, you can't just set fire to anything you fancy, see.

Lou the Lighter Yeah boss. But she looked at me funny.

Da Boss Overlord: Say, she is your stepmother. They all do that. Say, if I set fire to everyone who ever looked at me funny, half our city would be in flames, see.

Lou the Lighter sniggering: Yeah, but I'm a Firestarter, a sometimes twisted one.

Da Boss Overlord: Say, look. I'm a reasonable criminal overlord, and in this case, burning her alive in her house, I can excuse. It's the other matter that I can't abide, see.

Lou the Lighter: Collecting credits for the children's hospital?

Da Boss Overlord: Do you see collecting for charities aligning with our family values?

The Overlord points to a framed e-screen on the wall marked 'family values' which clearly reads—
'All for one and Da Boss gets all, comprendere?'

Da Boss Overlord turns to his guards: Say, cut off his hands then toss him off the roof. Nothing I despise more than a do-gooder, see. Your late father would be ashamed of the man you turned into.

Lou the Lighter: But what about the children?

Da Boss Overlord: Say, and guards, don't forget to burn down that hospital while you're at it.

One of the Carlos approached Da Boss Overlord and whispered something in his ear as Lou the Lighter was being dragged out.

"Say, my new favourite entertainment consultants, back on schedule as promised." Vinnie Da Boss turned his attention to them.

"You see brother. This is why I don't donate to charities. It's bad for one's pocket, as well as one's health." Nickolas smiled as he stepped forward and gave the Da Boss a half bow.

"Say, I like the cut of you two's fabric. And if things go down later like they should, I'm sure I could find room in my organisation for the two of you. Say, now have a seat gents, and we will have a few drinks and discuss the great blight of the wheels of time, see." Da Boss motioned for them to sit at some large nearby couches.

A fair while later, and a few great blights of the wheel of time resolved — along with a great many refreshments — Nickolas' communicator lit up, which Jonathan insisted he pick up.

"What is it Beeksy, we are a tad busy here. I trust you are almost finished," Nickolas said impatiently as he finished another drink and motioned for more.

Yes, almost there. But I think you need to come down here and look at the markings on these rockets. We *need* to run some safety checks or who knows what might happen. Granted, I don't have much experience with—" Berkley's audio was cut off mid-sentence.

"Let me cut you off there, Beeksy, to tell you what an outstandingly mediocre job you are doing. Now, complete the task at hand. Then you can take a load off. We will handle it from there. Over and out!" Nickolas then terminated the transmission.

"Say, everything on schedule, gentleman?" Da Boss enquired.

"Yes. Seems we even have spare time to consider running some dry runs and safety checks." Nickolas smiled.

"Dry Runs? Safety checks? Hilarious! Say, now get my two guests some more drinks!" Da Boss commanded as he and his entire entourage broke out laughing.

"Thanks, your holiness. We will take them to go as we have a p-p-p-p-party to start!!" Beamed Nickolas.

T-1 Bang!

"IT'S GO TIME!"

The celebrations couldn't be going any better. The light show was now in full swing with the loud music and 7D lighting beams bouncing off the outpost's buildings and now partly opened dome walls all working in perfect unison with the fireworks launched from the *Beletheia* as it hovered above the city. The residents were also having some type of victory parade down the main street, although it did feel a little forced given all the dodgy locals pointing weapons at each other as they marched towards an open courtyard directly below Vinnie Da Boss Overlord's balcony.

On the bridge of the *Beletheia,* the brothers were watching the monitors. "Look sharp people. It's show time." Even Nickolas was mildly excited at this point.

"What sodding bloody people?" Jonathan looked behind him.

Vinnie Da Boss Overlord walked out onto his balcony dressed in flowing black robes with a massive crown perched on his head to address the people below. M011y was mildly satisfied as she abruptly ended the light show, replacing it instantly with a solitary light shining directly onto the Overlord himself.

Da Boss Overlord: Greetings, salutations, and welcome to the inaugural national celebration of the newly formed 'Vinnie's Empire'.

Canned applause emanated from speakers strategically located throughout the, let's just say, less than enthusiastic crowd below.

Da Boss Overlord: Now it's not entirely your fault that we haven't celebrated victory over the Gambunyepio family before now. But it mostly is, see.

Canned agreement now emanated from the speakers below.

Da Boss Overlord: See, yah are what yah are in this galaxy. That's either one of two things: Either you're somebody, or you ain't nobody. And I ain't nobody, see.

Canned agreement then applause.

Da Boss Overlord: Say, and another thing, it's my birth-cycle so I expect respect and gifts aplenty for rulin' you rabble, see?

The Overlord's speech was disrupted by the sound of multiple 'gifts' masquerading as laser fire, originating from the crowd below, bouncing off Da Boss's protective laser-proof shield.

Da Boss Overlord: You're all trash, see, *but* as a sign of my respect, please try and dodge my guard's laser fire long enough to see that no-good Gambunyepio family's flagship blown apart.

Canned ooooooooOOOOOOOOHHHHHHHHhhhhooooo!

Da Boss Overlord: Good moon-cycle to you all!

Da Boss lifted his arms slowly for maximum effect, then shouted in a triumphant tone, "Power!"

"Okay! That's the signal. It's GO time!" Nickolas hit a big red button on the weapons control console.

Initially, there was no sound, which made everyone nervous. Nickolas, thinking the firing button was faulty, started pressing it more frantically.

A few moments later though, the entire planet's population could hear a faint rumbling sound from the ground. The sound gradually getting louder and louder, and a few in the courtyard crowd looked visibly nervous.

"Did all the missiles jolly well launch?" Jonathan asked.

"Acc0rding t0 weapons control, yes," M011y replied in a bored tone.

"So, where the sodding hell did they go?" Jonathan asked somewhat anxiously.

"D0wnwards," she answered phlegmatically.

Nickolas startled. "What do you mean?"

"I mean. You f00l, they *went into* the planet itself." M011y brought up a map of 100 missiles boring their way quite happily towards the planet's core.

"M011y er … might you do us proud by moving the ship a bit

further away from the planet."

"Already on it." M011y moved the ship a lot further away from Zertion 11.

The bad feeling on Zertion's surface had now started to spread and turned quickly into panic as the loud rumble below resulted in a few minor earth-tremors and the odd building shaking.

Then, deadly quiet.

"Phew, thought old Muck-a-muck here and friends were in trouble there." Nickolas half-grinned at his brother as he turned his attention elsewhere.

A few moments later, Jonathan, who was still watching the monitors intently broke the silence.

"Er … brother … you might be right. It might in-fact be jolly GO! time after all." Jonathan's shaking hands motioned for his twin to refocus his attention on the planet below.

T-0 Golly Gosh

"LOOK, I ADMIT. MISTAKES WERE MADE."

The Milarum twins had box seats to the spectacle as the *Beletheia*, still hovering in low orbit, had a panoramic view as the ice planet, Zertion 11, began to violently rip apart right before their eyes. Adding to the drama, the light and sound show was still emanating its hefty beats from the partially open and now cracked protective dome. This was certainly adding to the ratings, as the images of what was transpiring were still being livestreamed across the entire sector.

As the twins continued to watch in awe, then horror, as the planet split in two. Ironically, the only object that seemed to remain in one piece was the Gambunyepio spacecraft they were commissioned to destroy.

"Wow! Whatever just happened really makes you think." Nickolas looked thoughtful.

"Do you jolly well mean that?" Jonathan asked.

"Nah! M011y, you might want to kill that lightshow now please, and the livestream. I'm guessing the residents have more pressing issues to attend to, like scrambling for their lives." But even Nickolas winced at the sight of the Da Boss Overlord's HQ getting sucked down a sinkhole created by the earthquakes.

"Right, after I send the jailbreak c0des to that Gambunyepio ship, and send it h0me," M011y said, who had more regard for the spaceship than the silly fools who thought that they controlled them.

"Golly gosh, crumbs, and golly gosh again." Jonathan was still taking in the sheer scale of the destruction.

"Golly gosh indeed. M011y, reach out to Beeksy would you? I think we have a few questions to ask our little apprentice," Nickolas said calmly, given the circumstances.

"L0cated him. Patching him in n0w." The primary viewing screen lit up with the image of Berkley dodging and weaving his way throughout the city, which was clearly crumbling around him.

"What in the blazers happened?" Nickolas shouted.

"You did point the missiles towards the target, old boy?" Jonathan added.

"This isn't my fault, it's yours. I tried to warn you, but you didn't listen," Berkley cried to the background sound of multiple buildings crumbling.

"Dear, poor Beeksy. We don't promote a blame culture here at IAFE. I'm afraid this might reflect badly on your career prospects." Nickolas shook his head in disappointment.

"What does positioning missiles have to do with entertaining children?" Berkley shouted as he continued to run for his life to the sound of rumbling and screaming in the background.

"Look, I'm sure it was covered in the induction somewhere. Anyway, stop running and confirm your location to M011y, she will transport you up," Nickolas added blandly.

"No thanks. And what's more, I resign. I'd rather take my chances down here than spend another moment with you two loonies," Berkley shouted.

"How rude! And after all we have done for you," Nickolas replied.

"Well let's just recap, shall we? In the two short sun-cycles I have been in your employ, I have just about been cut in half, abused, threatened, shot, chased, stolen weapons of mass destruction, and now, it seems, helped destroy an entire planet. Have I missed anything?" Berkley yelled.

"Probably, but quite the ride huh," Nickolas beamed.

"Oh! Up yoooouuuuurrrrr …zzzzzzzzttttppp—" The last image of Berkley making a rude gesture started flickering, then disappeared altogether.

"Poor Berkley. It seems we have lost transmission." Jonathan made a half-arsed attempt to regain contact.

"Yeah, shame. But can't be helped. Right, M011y get us out of here," Nickolas commanded.

M011y had to make some smooth moves around bits of Zertion 11 as it hurtled into space, but the *Beletheia* was now clear of the planetary remains and any danger.

"Inc0ming c0mmunicat1on," M011y announced as the image of a cat-like creature filled the primary viewing screen.

"Fredrick old boy! How jolly nice to see you. How are you? You look … well?" Jonathan trailed off as the image of a clearly worse for wear Fredrick lit up the screen.

"Oh! Shut it dude. I'm in a foul mood already. Head back to HQ immediately," Fredrick said.

"Why are you soaking wet? And why are your hands bandaged up?" Nickolas laughed.

"Look dudes. Just get back here pronto. Felicity wants to see you both urgently," Fredrick wasn't going to be drawn into an explanation.

"Jolly good." Jonathan turned and whispered to Nickolas, "Word couldn't have travelled that fast, could it?" His brother shrugged.

"What word? What have you dudes done now?" Fredrick sounded suspicious.

"Tell Felicity we will be along shortly. We just have some jolly admin work to attend to first. Transmission out." Jonathan cut Fredrick off before he could table any of the 300 questions he now had.

"Admin? Oh yeah, thanks for reminding me. M011y, please send our invoice through to Da Boss Overlord's accounts department. Assuming, at least, some of the department would have survived the celebration, right?" Nickolas said calmly as he handed the still trembling hands of his twin his newly created cocktail the

Max Effect of a LightBridge[12].

"Have you gone completely blotto!" Jonathan looked at his brother in disbelief.

"Look, I admit. Mistakes were made. But I feel, in the end, this latest learning experience will only make us stronger, together." Nickolas smirked, then took another sip of his cocktail.

"Then u Nick0las 'Muck-a-muck' Milarum must be the str0ngest being in the entire un1verse," M011y stated sarcastically as the *Beletheia* fired up its engines and set course for IAFE HQ, Aertion 82.

---

[12] 27 parts of 100-proof fermented potato.

2 parts rocket fuel (it has got to be the good blue stuff).

1 part of that candy that pops (not explodes) in your mouth.

Max Effect quickly became the go to cocktail whenever attending a Planet Exploding Viewing (PEV) party in the Outer Brim. Ironically the licensing royalties alone for this cocktail would have made the twins wealthy if they ever remembered to trademark the recipe. This omission was no doubt due to the little-known side effect that popping candy could cause short term memory loss with certain species.

T–00 But Wait, There's More...

"WHY END THERE?"
Coming November, 2024

Preorder at:
https://www.amazon.com.au/stores/Richard-H-Polden/author/B076BBXTHH

For all things R.H. Polden and bonus content go to
https://polden.io/